Dear mouse friends,
Welcome to the world of

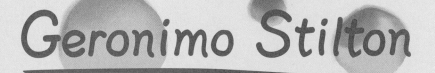

Geronimo Stilton

THE RODENT'S GAZETTE
EDITORIAL STAFF

Geronimo Stilton
A learned and brainy
mouse; editor of
The Rodent's Gazette

Thea Stilton
Geronimo's sister and
special correspondent at
The Rodent's Gazette

Trap Stilton
An awful joker;
Geronimo's cousin and
owner of the store
Cheap Junk for Less

Benjamin Stilton
A sweet and loving
nine-year-old mouse;
Geronimo's favorite
nephew

Geronimo Stilton

I'M NOT A SUPERMOUSE!

Scholastic Inc.

New York   Toronto   London   Auckland

Sydney   Mexico City   New Delhi   Hong Kong

ISBN 978-0-545-10375-6

Copyright © 2008 by Edizioni Piemme S.p.A., Via Tiziano 32, 20145 Milan, Italy.

International Rights © Atlantyca S.p.A.

English translation © 2010 by Atlantyca S.p.A.

Based on an original idea by Elisabetta Dami.

www.geronimostilton.com

Published by Scholastic Inc., 557 Broadway, New York, NY 10012. SCHOLASTIC and associated logos are trademarks and/or registered trademarks of Scholastic Inc.

Stilton is the name of a famous English cheese. It is a registered trademark of the Stilton Cheese Makers' Association. For more information, go to www.stiltoncheese.com

Text by Geronimo Stilton
Original title *Non sono un supertopo!*
Cover by Giuseppe Ferrario
Illustrations by Elena Tomasutti and Christian Aliprandi
Graphics by Merenguita Gingermouse and Yuko Egusa

Special thanks to Beth Dunfey
Translated by Lidia Morson Tramontozzi
Interior design by Kay Petronio

12 11 10 9   13 14 15 16/0

Printed in the U.S.A.   40
First printing, October 2010

A MOUSE TRAP

Hello! My name is Stilton, *Geronimo Stilton*. What you're about to read is one of my favorite **ADVENTURES**. You see, I just love reading. In fact, this particular story began because of a book. . . .

It was a beautiful Saturday afternoon in *spring*, and I was whistling *HAPPILY* as I strolled along the streets of New Mouse City. I was in a good mood because I'd planned a really nice day. First, I'd shop for some fresh cheese, then I'd head over to **New Mouse City's library**, where the library mouse was holding a **book** for me. It was something I'd wanted to read for a **LONG** time.

When I was done with my shopping, I scurried over to the library. After chatting with the library mouse, I checked out the book.

The security guard shouted, "**The library is closing!** All rodents are kindly asked to get their books and leave the premises!"

I scampered onto the elevator and pushed the DOWN **button**. The elevator began going down. But suddenly, between the third and second floors, I heard a **SCREECH**, and the elevator came to a dead **STOP**. The lights went out, and I was plunged into **DARKNESS**.

I waited for a moment, then squeaked at the

top of my lungs: "Help! The **elevator** is stuck!"

There was no response. A **chill** ran down my tail as a TERRIFYING thought struck me: "I'm stuck in an elevator on a Saturday afternoon and no one has a clue I'm here!"

Cold sweat dripped from my whiskers. My head was spinning like a **mousey-go-round** at an amusement park. My heart was racing **FASTER** than a gerbil on a treadmill. I banged my paws on the steel doors, screaming, "**HELP**, I'm traaaapppppped!"

Despite the **darkness**, I saw something move. "**AAAAAAAAARRRRRRRGGHH!**" I screeched.

Then I looked closer: It was only my own REFLECTION in the elevator's mirror!

A REAL, TRUE EMERGENCY!

I tried to get a **grip**. I began to think things through.

"OK, it's Saturday afternoon. The **library** will reopen on Monday morning. So I'll just wait **calmly** until then."

But the thought of being stuck in an elevator for a day and a half gave me a bad case of **scaredy-mouse syndrome**. I began to sob, **"HEEEELP! HEEEELP!"**

There was no response.

I sighed, then sat down. I figured I might as well make myself comfortable. I needed to **cheer up** a bit, so I rummaged through my shopping bags

and found a piece of **cheese**. I began munching on it slowly, then drank a sip of **orange juice**. It was lucky I'd just done my shopping: A piece of cheese usually calms me down right away. After all, what mouse doesn't **love** cheese?

For a moment, I felt better. How bad could it be? I had food to eat and a juicy book to entertain me. I'd planned on spending the whole weekend **reading** anyway.

Too bad it was so **DARK** in here!

In fact, it was **pitch-black**. All that **darkness** reminded me I hate small spaces. I get really claustrophobic!

I took a deep breath. There was nothing to do but wait. So I removed my jacket, folded it into a **pillow**, curled up my **tail**, and tried to **sleep**. A nap was a surefire way to pass the time.

But no matter how much I tried, I just couldn't seem to **relax**. Maybe it was the darkness. Maybe it was the stuffiness. Maybe it was my own 'fraidy-ness. Whatever it was, I **TOSSED** and **turned** for hours.

When I finally fell asleep, I had terrible dreams. I dreamed I'd been buried alive in a **MUMMY'S TOMB**. It was my most **BONE-CHILLING** nightmare ever!

Sunday morning finally rolled around. I couldn't see the **sun**, of course, but I realized it was morning when I checked the fluorescent light on my **watch**.

By this time, I was starting to feel like the cheese had slipped off my cracker. I tried to *comfort* myself by humming **softly**. I wrapped my tail around myself and rocked back and forth, squeaking to myself.

After a few hours of that, I heard a ring.

Rriiiiiiiiiiiiiiiing!!!

I jumped up. What was that? Something was **vibrating** inside my pocket!

Vrrrrrrrrrrrrrrrrrrrrrrr!

I smacked myself on the snout. **Holey cheese!** It was my **cell phone**!

And to think I considered myself a brainy mouse! Why hadn't I remembered it sooner? With trembling paws, I grabbed the phone and sobbed, "H-hello? I-I'm a CHEESEBRAIN. . . . I mean, I'm G-Geronimo. . . . I'm elevator in a stuck. . . . I mean, I'm stuck in an elevator! Please get me **OOOOOUUUUUUT**!!!!"

My cell phone! Why hadn't I remembered it sooner?

HYENA HERE,
BRUCE HYENA!

A loud, **HEARTY** squeak roared back at me,
"Hello, Hyena here. Bruce Hyena!"

"B-B-Bruce," I stammered. "I'm so glad
you called. I'm trapped in an elevator, in the
dark. . . . I'm scared and —"

He cut me short in his usual **aBRuPt** way.
"Pipe down, Cheesehead! Where are you?"

"Umm, in an elevator in the New Mouse
City Public Library. . . ."

Bruce heaved a **sigh**.

"I'll be right there, Cheese Puff!"

I smiled. Bruce was one of my dearest
friends. He was a really **brawny** mouse —
just the rodent you'd want by your side in an
EMERGENCY.

I didn't know
how he'd do it.
But one thing was certain:
Bruce would get me

OUT

of here right away!
If there's one thing
I knew about him . . .

THE THOUSAND FACES OF BRUCE HYENA

He's a parachutist who throws himself into every adventure!

He always protects nature.

He can sail a sailboat.

Ain't no mountain high enough for him!

He has a great sense of direction, so he never gets lost.

He loves to sing and tell stories around the campfire.

He has one secret: He loves romantic novels and poetry.

A few minutes later, I heard **some paws** run up the stairs. Then **some paws** pounded furiously on the elevator doors. Finally, **somebody** exclaimed, "Don't worry! **Everything is under control!**"

I whispered, "Bruce, is that you?"

No one answered. The elevator doors **creaked** open. A sliver of **light** shone through. I blinked a few times. It had been a long time since I'd seen daylight.

LIGHT! AIR! FREEDOM!

Then an iron paw pulled me through the gap in the doors. **Somebody** shouted in my ear, "Everything OK, **CHAMP**?"

I barely managed to **SQUEAK**. Then I **passed out**.

I Thought I'd Leave My Fur There!

I spent the rest of the day at home, resting. A nice **HOT** bath, some tasty **cheese**, and a good night's **sleep** quickly restored me.

The next day, I told everybody in the office about my **unlucky** adventure. Oh, excuse me, I almost forgot to tell you — I run *The Rodent's Gazette*, the biggest newspaper in New Mouse City.

"I was so scared!" I sighed. "Alone all night in the elevator, in the dark. . . . I thought I'd leave my FUR there forever!"

My sister THEA snorted. "No chance of leaving anything there, except maybe your common sense! You just spent a night in an elevator, that's all!"

"If it were me, I would have just taken a nice ratnap," my cousin Trap snickered. "If life gives you cheese, make a triple-decker sandwich! Know what I mean?"

Bruce was quiet. He put a paw on me and said seriously, "Tell me, Cheesehead, why didn't you call me right away?"

"Actually . . . hmm . . . I didn't think of it," I admitted. "I don't know why."

Bruce nodded. Then he shouted in my ear: "I'll tell you why, Cheese Puff! Because you're a BUNDLE of nerves! Because you LOST

YOUR COOL! Because you panicked!"

He **pinched** my ear. "OUUUCCHHH!" I shrieked.

Bruce ignored me. "Remember these **golden** rules:

> RULE NO. 1: ALWAYS KEEP CALM!
> RULE NO. 2: BE QUICK ON YOUR PAWS!
> RULE NO. 3: LEARN TO ADAPT!
> RULE NO. 4: BE AWARE OF YOUR SURROUNDINGS!

"Got it, **CHAMP**?"

He scribbled something in a small orange notebook, then slammed it shut. He nodded, gave my sister a **high five** (why?), **WINKED** at my cousin (why?), and signaled Benjamin not to worry (why, why, why?).

Bruce turned to look me in the snout. "I've got just the **cure** for what ails you," he declared. "*Just you wait!*"

Bruce grabbed my tail and dragged me up the stairs to the roof. An orange **helicopter** was waiting for us.

Naturally, I refused to get in. I'd been on enough of Bruce's ADVENTURES to know better than to go anywhere with him. I **struggled** valiantly, but in the end, an *intellectual* mouse like me couldn't compete with Bruce's **MASSIVE** muscles. He picked me up and **THREW** me in.

Help!

Just you wait!

A PLACE WITH LOTS AND LOTS OF SAND

Bruce gave me a pair of MIRRORED sunglasses, just like his. "Put these on! Under the seat you'll find a backpack stuffed with everything we need for where we're going."

Now I was really worried. Why was he being so mysterious? "Soooo, where are we going?"

Bruce chuckled. "Let's play a GAME, CHAMP. You like games, don't you?"

I smiled nervously. I do like games, but mostly of the board variety.

"See if you can guess," Bruce continued. "It's a place with lots and lots of sand."

"The **beach**?" I breathed **hopefully**.

He snorted. "A **beach**? YOU WISH, Cheesehead!"

I tried again. "The **HaMSTeR ISLaNDS**?"

"Where we're going is much, much, much **BIGGER** than an island, **CHAMP**!" he declared. "In fact, it's almost four million square miles! It's very, very, very **hot** there. It gets up to **one hundred degrees** Fahrenheit in the shade! And it's very, very, very DRY. It never rains!"

I was **INCREDULOUS**. "A place like that doesn't exist. . . ."

He snickered. "You should see how the **sun** shines. It's so **hot**, you could get a **tan** in the middle of the night!"

I was beginning to have a **bad** feeling about this. But Bruce was laughing very hard.

Once he caught his breath, he said, "There

are lots and lots and lots of **camels**!"

I was flabbergasted. "Wh-what?? What do camels have to do with anything?"

Bruce was **rolling with laughter** in the helicopter, making it **BOUNCE** up and down. I clutched my stomach. You see, I have a bad history of **MOTION SiCKNESS**.

WE WERE SWINGING UP AND DOWN . . . UP AND DOWN . . . UP AND DOWN . . .

"Look down," Bruce sputtered between laughs. "There are the **camels**!"

Below us was a blanket of sand.
It was veryveryvery **big** . . .
veryveryvery **hot** . . .
and veryveryvery **dry** . . .
with lots and lots and lots of **camels**!

Bruce had finally gotten control of himself. "I bet you're wondering where the **beach** is, right?" He burst out laughing again.

But that was no **beach**. It was **the Sahara Desert**!

"If you don't lather yourself up with sunblock from the tip of your *tail* to the tip of your **whiskers**, you'll be in agony!" he bellowed. "Out here, you need a sunblock that's **SPF 1000**!"

"But **SPF 1000** sunblock doesn't exist!" I stammered.

"Exaaaaaaaactly! So stay in the **SHADE** as much as you can, otherwise you'll be a **ROASTED RODENT**! Now, get ready. Your **tests** are about to begin!"

Tests? **What tests?** I sighed. Well, at least I was good at tests. . . .

THE DESERT

What is a desert?

A desert is an area that is almost completely uninhabited, where it hardly ever rains, and where the terrain is arid and infertile.

Some deserts are **hot deserts**. These deserts are made up of mostly rock or sand. Strong winds create big sand **dunes**.

There are also **cold deserts**, like those in Greenland, the Arctic, and the Antarctic. Cold deserts are huge expanses of snow and ice, where the chill is intense and truly brutal!

The Sahara

The **Sahara** is the largest non-polar desert in the word. It's in northern Africa, and it occupies an area of about **3,475,000 square miles**.

It is a huge stretch of sand marked by traces of ancient rivers. When it rains (which happens rarely!), they fill up with water. In some areas, water springs from below the ground, forming a rich area of vegetation called an **oasis**.

The Sahara is home to desert tribes like the **Tuareg**. These nomadic people devote themselves mostly to agriculture and shepherding. They are easily recognizable because, to protect themselves from the sun, they wear a blue headpiece and long, colorful clothes with wide sleeves.

THE TESTS!!!

"OK, it's time for your **tests**," Bruce announced. "In a little while, I'll make a **real mouse** out of you!"

I could feel my whiskers **trembling** with terror. "I don't need to become a **real mouse**. I'm happy just the way I am!" I declared.

Bruce shook his snout. "That's where you're **wrong**. It's not safe for you to remain the way you are. Look at what happened in the elevator! You're too **wimpy**! You need to hone your instincts and get in touch with the **real mouse** inside you, Champ! Don't worry about it, though. I'll take care of everything! You can thank me later. Now . . . **it's time for test number one**!"

Before I realized what was happening, Bruce reached over toward my collar.

"Uh-oh, what do we have here? Lookie here, Cheesehead. It's a **SCORPION**!"

I let out an *ear-piercing* scream. "A scorpioooooooooooon? Heeeeeeeeeeeeelp!"

Bruce just **LAUGHED**. He swung the **SCORPION** back and forth in front of my snout. "Don't worry, **CHAMP**! It's made of rubber!" Then he said more seriously: "**Rule No. 1: Always keep calm!** If it had been real, you'd be **catmeat** by now!"

After my heart stopped pounding, I started **chasing** him. "**BRUUUUCEE!** When I catch you, you'll see how calm I can be!"

As he **scampered** away from me, Bruce headed up a huge dune with SAND as fine as powder. Once he reached the **top**, he started taunting me.

"Come on, **Cheese Puff**, show me what you've got! I want to see you **flex** those muscles! Lift those paws, **HOP, HOP**!"

I tried to lift my paws, but as I plodded up the dune, each paw **sank** into the sand.

Aaahhhhhhhh!

When I got to the top, Bruce tripped me.

"I'm doing this for you, **Cheesehead**!" he shouted. **"One day you'll thank me."**

As I rolled down the dune, he shouted, "That's no good at all! You've failed the **test**. You forgot **Rule No. 2: Be quick on your paws!**"

There was SAND in my clothes and fur! While I was trying to shake it off, Bruce **scurried** down the hill and pawed me some **CHEESE**. "Now, eat this! I'm doing it for your own good. **One day you'll thank me.**"

One day? I was ready to thank him right now — I was **starving**! I opened my mouth to take a big bite when I noticed the cheese was covered with **WORMS**! **"EEWWWWWW!"** I shrieked. I threw it away in disgust.

Bruce shook his snout. "No good at all! **Cheesehead**, you botched the test. You forgot **Rule No. 3: Learn to adapt!** If **wormy cheese** is all you have to eat, then eat **wormy cheese**!"

The next morning, I woke at dawn.

I **stretched**, scratched my whiskers, then sat bolt upright: I was ALONE in the tent except for this note!

> TEST No. 4: MEET ME AT THE OASIS!
> WALK EAST FOR TWO HOURS, THEN GO WEST. ONE DAY YOU'LL THANK ME!

Thank Bruce? Thanking him was the **FURTHEST** thing from my mind! How could I make it on my own in the **DESERT**? And where was the **OASIS**? I had **no idea**!

However, I soon realized I had no choice but to do as Bruce said. I couldn't stay in the tent alone. I had only the **clothes** on my back and a small amount of **FOOD** and **WATER** in my backpack. So I started out.

It turned out to be one of the most horrible

days of my life. I tried to figure out where I was, but there were no points of reference! There was **nothing** in the desert. Only

SAND... SAND... SAND...
SAND... SAND... AND MORE SAND.

As the sun began to set, I noticed something familiar on the ground. I realized it was my pawkerchief. That meant I had already been there! I was going in circles!

I started to sob. "I'm loooooost! I'm scared!"

Just then, Bruce came from behind a dune and yelled, "No good at all, **Cheesehead**! You **FLUNKED** this test, too. Remember Rule No. 4: Be aware of your surroundings!"

Bruce led me to a tree at the OASIS. "You're probably wondering why I brought you here, aren't you?" Bruce asked kindly.

"Er, yes. **Why** did you bring me here?"

"Geronimo, I'm going to give you a very VALUABLE piece of advice," Bruce said seriously. *"Be quiet* and **DON'T MOVE**!"

I was about to ask why, when I heard a faint buzzing that grew louder and LOUDER!

A second later, I was covered with bees! That was weird! Yet here they were, ALL OVER tHE PLACE! They were crawling on my ears, whiskers, and nose! There were bees from my glasses down to my tail.

Bees! Bees!! Bees! Bees! Bees! Bees! Bees!! Bees! Bees! Bees!

What a **NIGHTMARE**!

Bruce clicked his stopwatch. "You're so LUCKY! This is a unique opportunity to measure how long you can keep cool. I'm going to count the seconds before you start SCREAMING. Ready, **Cheesehead**? One . . . Two . . . Three . . . CONGRATULATIONS, so far . . . Nine . . . Ten . . . Why haven't you screamed? Fifteen . . . Sixteen . . . Did I **mention** if you **scream**, you'll get STUNG?"

DESERT BEES

It may seem strange, but in some areas of the desert, where water is plentiful and plants thrive (such as oases), bees can live and produce honey.

DISAPPOINTED, Bruce muttered, "Hmm, you're not screaming!"

I didn't scream because I was too afraid to! I had no **INTENTION** of getting stung.

But Bruce had more tricks up his **fur**. "Fine!" he shouted. "I guess I'll have to make the **test** harder!"

He snickered, then shook the tree trunk until the bees' nest fell **right on my head**!

Now those bees were really mad! They **SWARMED** around me so thickly, I couldn't see my own snout. I **ran** away, and they began to **chase** me!

Bzzzzzzzzzzzzzzzzzzzzzzzzzzz!

I ran to the pond in the middle of the **oasis** and dove in snout-first.

"GOOD FOR YOU!" Bruce shouted. "Record time: 325 feet in nine seconds!"

TOO DARN HOT!

I dragged myself to the tent, threw myself on the cot, and promptly fell asleep. The night (which was **frigid**, like all nights in the desert!) was very short. It felt like I was **asleep** for only five minutes when a **SCREECH** jolted me awake.

"Get up, **Cheese Puff**! Get to!"

"W-w-what? Where am I?" I stuttered.

A minute later, it all came **FLOODING** back. I knew exactly where I was: in the desert, with Bruce. I peeked out of the tent just as the **sun** was rising in a cloudless sky.

"How **beautiful**!" I breathed.

Unfortunately, that *peaceful* moment was just that — a moment. Seconds after the sun peeked above the horizon, Bruce leaned over

DESERT SURVIVAL GEAR

**SNAKE AND SCORPION
ANTIVENOM KIT**

**WATER BOTTLE
AND DRINK MIX**

**BANDAGES
FOR BLISTERS**

**MIRRORED
SUNGLASSES**

ENERGY BARS

HIKING BOOTS

SUNBLOCK

FLASHLIGHT

SUN HAT

THERMOS

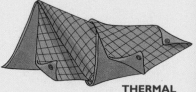

**THERMAL
TENT**

and *shouted* in my ear, "Show's over, Cheese Puff! It's time to WARM UP your puny little **muscles** with some exercise!"

Oh, we **warmed up**, all right! Fifteen minutes later, I was HOTTER than an overcooked grilled cheese sandwich!

But that wasn't enough for Bruce. He

kept giving me more and more challenging exercises while the temperature kept rising.

After **one** hour, it was HOT!

After **two** hours, it was SWELTERING!

Keep at it, Cheesehead!

Ugh!

After **three** hours, it was SCORCHING!

After that, I don't remember a thing. MY brain was fried!

The **whole day** was like that. Bruce gave me one exercise routine after another, even when the desert sun was HIGH IN THE SKY and beating down mercilessly. He had me do floor exercises, running, bending, jumping, weight lifting, and the worst of the bunch: He made me STARVE all day long!

As I sweated away, he squeaked at me ruthlessly. "Come on, CHAMP! Are you a REAL MOUSE or a *cheese puff*?"

I did my best not to look like a cheese puff, but it was hard! The sun was ROASTING!

At the end of the day, I was completely cooked. Bruce took one look at my BURNED snout and BURST OUT laughing. "Good for you, CHAMP! You're making progress.

You don't look like a cheese puff anymore —
you look more like a BAKED CHEESE
PUFF!"

He dragged me off to the tent. I was so
relieved. I couldn't wait to curl into a
furball and fall asleep.

"Don't worry, Cheesehead. I have a **nice
surprise** lined up for you for tomorrow,"
Bruce told me as he tucked me in.

"Really?" I mumbled wearily. And with
that small RAY of hope, I fell asleep.

It's too darn hot!

TOO DARN COLD!

At dawn the next day, Bruce woke me up with his usual hearty squeak:

"**On your paws, Cheesehead.** Wake up and get going! I have a surprise for you. We're leaving!"

I was on my paws in an *instant*. I couldn't **wait** to get out of there! I folded my sleeping bag, stuffed it into my backpack, and zipped it up in a jiffy. Things were looking **up**! My woes were finally coming to an end.

Oh, how **wrong** I was!

I heard the roar of an engine outside our tent. Bruce was waiting for me in the orange **HELICOPTER**.

As soon as I'd scrambled on board, Bruce leaned over and shouted, "Let's play a game.

See if you can guess where I'm taking you. You're **HOT**, right?"

"You can say that again! This place is hotter than **Roasted Rat Volcano** on the Fourth of July!"

Bruce nodded. "So you'd like to go someplace *nice and cool*, right?"

"Oh, yes!" I said **EAGERLY**. "That sounds perfect!"

Bruce rubbed his snout *thoughtfully*. "Well, I happen to know a spot like that. How does that sound, **CHAMP**?"

Throwing caution to the wind, I answered, "Sure! The **cooler** the better!"

Bruce smiled from ear to ear. "OK, now let's see if you can guess where I'm thinking of. It's a little place that's far, far, **far away**. It's scarcely **INHABITED**, and very WINDY. . . ."

I shrugged. "Someplace WINDY . . . um, I have

no idea. Come on, Bruce, just tell me. **WHERE** are you taking me? Where are we **GOING**?"

Bruce **howled** with satisfaction. "You're going to love this place, Champ! It's the coolest spot on Earth! **MOUNTAINS** of snow, **FROZEN** rivers, temperatures one hundred degrees **BELOW ZERO**. That's right, we're going to the *Nooooorth Pooooole!*"

"**The North Pole?**" I screeched. "I'd rather stay here!"

Bruce put his paw on the gas. "Oh, no you don't, **Cheese Puff**! A **REAL MOUSE** doesn't change his mind every five minutes, depending on which way the wind is blowing. You already said you preferred the **COLD**. So cold it is!"

It was a gruesome trip. After the helicopter, we took a **PLANE**, then an **ICE CHOPPER**, then another **HELICOPTER**. . . .

HEAVY SCARF

LINED GLOVES

SNOUT MASK WITH INSULATED LINING

BARRIER SKIN CREAM*

BREATHABLE WATER-PROOF JACKET

TRIPLE-LAYER WOOL SWEATER

EARMUFFS

GLASSES FOR THE WIND, FOG, AND SUN

WATERPROOF TAIL COVER

BREATHABLE WATERPROOF PANTS

HIKING BOOTS

HEAVY WOOL SOCKS

SNOWSHOES

NORTH POLE SURVIVAL KIT

* *Barrier skin cream insulates the skin from the cold. It also protects the skin from chapping caused by freezing temperatures.*

The entire time, Bruce rattled off to me INSTRUCTIONS on how to survive in temperatures a hundred degrees below zero.

"First of all, CHEESEHEAD, remember not to sweat. If you do, your sweat will freeze on you!"

"That's it!" I protested. "I'm going home. That way I won't sweat for sure. . . ."

"Oh, no you don't!" Bruce scolded. "You're in my capable paws now, Cheese Puff! What you need is self-control! Don't worry. I'll teach you everything you need to know to survive."

He made me dress in polar gear — THREE LAYERS of everything, from my hat down to my socks! When I finally got off the helicopter, I had so many items of clothes on, I could hardly move. I looked like the Abominable Snowrat!

I looked around in despair. We were in a borderless desert of ice, also known as an ice pack.* It was bitterly **cold** — much **colder** than I could ever have imagined. I felt like I was trapped inside a **subzero** freezer!

"Did you put on some barrier skin cream, **CHEESEHEAD**?" Bruce asked. He had to shout to be heard over the frigid winds gusting around us.

"**Cream?** What cream?" I shouted back.

"The cream that protects against the cold and wind. You don't want your *whiskers* to freeze, do you?"

"Actually, I . . ."

"That's **BAD**, Cheddarface. They could **crumble** and fall right off!"

Oh no, not my *whiskers*! I got so stressed out, I could feel **little beads** of perspiration forming on my neck and back.

An ice pack is a sheet of ice that covers the sea. Ice packs are common in the polar regions.

Bruce has a sixth sense about these things. He gave me a look that would've scared a rabid tomcat. "You aren't **Sweating**, are you?" he demanded.

"**Wh-why do you ask?**" I stuttered nervously.

"Because you could **FREEZE** like a fish stick! By the way, did you put on your waterproof insulated **tail cover**?"

"My what?" I asked.

"That means no, right? That's very bad,

Cheese Puff. Your tail could freeze! You don't want it to **FALL OFF**, do you?"

My whiskers began to tremble. Not from the cold, but from *anxiety*! You see, I'm very attached to my tail. I shouted, "**It's too cold here! I want to go home!**"

Bruce slapped my shoulder. "Come on, Cheesehead! The **fun** has just begun!"

"**Fun? Fun?!**" I screeched. "You call this **fun**?!?!"

I want to go home!

Come on, Cheese Puff!
The fun has just begun!

Bruce gave me a pat on the back. "Come on, **CHAMP**! We're off to the **North Pole**! Think how much fun it'll be! We'll pull sleds carrying food and equipment for a good **HUNDRED MILES**, or until the **GPS*** tells us we've hit the North Pole. What could be **BETTER**? It's going to be an **AMAZING** adventure!"

I didn't bother answering. I started **PULLING** the sled in silence to conserve my energy. I thought: *The sooner we get to the North Pole, the sooner we'll leave this **DREADFUL** place!*

It was a **looooong**, grueling march. It seemed to go on **FOREVER**. All we saw all day long was **ICE**, **ICE**, and more **ICE**! I felt like I was becoming one with our surroundings, but not in a good way. I was frozen like a **MOUSICLE**! My whiskers were frozen,

---

**GPS stands for Global Positioning System. A GPS can pinpoint its user's exact location anywhere in the world.*

my tail was frozen, my fur was frozen, even my **GLASSES** were frozen!

At dusk on the seventh day, **we had arrived**! I collapsed in a frozen heap. I'd never been so **happy** to reach a destination.

"Good for you, **CHAMP**!" Bruce cheered. "When you don't **disappoint** me, you do me **proud**!"

Talk about faint words of **praise**!

A little while later, a motor roared above us. **HURRAH!** The orange **HELICOPTER** had come to get us.

Chop-chop, Cheesehead!
Move those paws!

Brrrr!

TOO MUCH JUNGLE!

As soon as we climbed on board the chopper, I curled up and fell asleep. I **slept** through the whole trip. I barely noticed when we changed transportation: helicopter, ship, plane, train, another ship, **another plane**. All I knew was that we were heading home. **What a fur-raising trip** it had been! I couldn't wait to be back in my nice, COZY mouse hole in New Mouse City.

While trying to catch a few **Z's**, I heard Bruce chattering away. I tried tuning him out, but I caught something about hungry **tigers**, the JUNGLE, **QUICKSAND**, and poisonous *snakes*. I guessed he was telling me a bedtime story. But I was so tired, I couldn't keep my eyes open.

JUNGLE SURVIVAL KIT

BOTTLE OF SNAKEBITE ANTIVENOM

CANTEEN

BUG-REPELLENT SPRAY

FLASHLIGHT

MACHETE

RAIN PONCHO

ROPE

THE JUNGLE

The jungle is a dense tangle of trees and vegetation at the heart of a tropical rain forest. Jungles are most common in the areas around the equator and the tropics. It rains frequently in the jungle, which helps the trees and bushes grow abundantly. Jungles are home to an unusually large percentage of animal species — some estimate that more than 50 percent of the world's species live in jungles.

It's always wise to wear light clothing in the jungle. It's also important to carry a survival kit with a few essential objects.

When I woke up, I was alone at the door to the plane. I heard Bruce yell in my ear, "OK, **CHEESEHEAD**, you were paying attention, right? If you want to stay alive, be sure to remember everything I told you. Now **OUT YOU GO**! You're going to have so much **fun**!"

HEEEEL P!!!

ROOOOAAR!

SLURP!

Bruce shoved me out of the plane and into . . . NOTHINGNESS! I fell for what seemed like an eternity. I started panicking, but then I remembered Bruce muttering something about a parachute. I felt around until I found a string, and I pulled it!

With a big rip, the parachute opened and

SMACK!

slowed my descent.

As I **WHIZZED** through the wind, I saw treetops below me coming closer and closer. . . .

I was headed straight for an extremely **DENSE** forest. . . .

No, actually . . .

IT WAS A JUNGLE!

Oh why, oh why hadn't I listened to Bruce's **babbling**? I should've known he would never be telling me something as **innocent** as a bedtime story! How was I ever going to **SURVIVE** in the **WILD JUNGLE**?

I'd barely had time to reflect on the **trouble I was in** when my parachute got tangled in the branches of a **HUMONGOUS** tree.

I sat quietly for a moment and took stock of the situation: I was lost in the jungle, tangled in a **parachute**, on top of a gigantically **TALL** tree.

"**HELP!**" I screamed. "I don't want to hang here like a **fly** waiting for a **spider!**"

I was in trouble. Real trouble!

As if being stuck in a tree wasn't enough to **scare the cheese** out of me, the jungle was full of terrifying sounds. First I thought I heard a pair of jaws opening and closing. . . . SMACK...

Maybe it was a hungry crocodile with **razor-sharp** teeth. . . .

SMACK...

Then I heard the **THUNDEROUS** roar of a tiger. . . .

ROOOOOAR!

Was it a ravenous Malaysian tiger? I shivered. I'd heard they love to eat rodents!

I couldn't think anymore. A cloud of insects was swarming around me. . . .

 Bzzzzzz! Bzzzzzz! Bzzzzzz! Bzzzzzz! Bzzzzzz!

Were they rare poisonous insects that could paralyze me with a single **bite**?

I trembled from the tip of my tail to the tip of my whiskers.

I screamed with every ounce of breath in my body, "Heeeeeeeeelp! Somebody help meeeeeeee!"

Nearby, I heard the rustling of leaves.

I sighed with relief. I knew it was Bruce. He'd come to save me!

But out of the **leaves**, a **HAIRY** face emerged! Then I saw two **beady** eyes and a protruding jaw.

I was a **goner**. It wasn't Bruce, it was an **ORANGUTAN**!

I was in deep, deep trouble!

The orangutan plucked me right out of the tree. She seemed happy to see me. She began **rocking** me gently, then a little **harder**. Eventually, she was rocking me so hard I felt seasick!

Then I **understood**! This was an **ORANGUTAN MOTHER**, and she'd mistaken me for one of her babies!

I cleared my throat **NERVOUSLY**. "Excuse me, ummm . . . **MRS. ORANGUTAN** . . . I think there's been a mistake. I **HATE** to disappoint you, but I'm not your son!"

She looked at me, a little puzzled. Then she began **picking through** the fur on my head. She was trying to find lice! Orangutans groom each other. They keep themselves clean by de-licing one another. It wasn't so bad, really, but — **OUCH!** — actually, it was a little **painful**!

"Please stop! I don't have any lice, I swear I don't! I'm not an **ORANGUTAN**, and I'm not your baby!"

But she continued examining my scalp as if I hadn't **squeaked** a word. Every now and then, she'd pluck some **tufts** of fur off my snout.

I finally had enough. "Please, I **BEG** you,

put me down and leave me alone! I just want to go home!"

At that, she picked me up and sat me on her knee. I think she was trying to calm me down, because she **forced** me to eat a bunch of bananas.

I'll have you know that I absolutely DESPISE bananas! This was **worse** than the desert. It was **worse** than the North Pole. Frankly, I didn't know how it could get any **worse** than this.

Just when I thought I couldn't take it anymore, who bursts out of the bushes? BRUCE!

"Hey, CHAMP, you shouldn't get too friendly with an orangutan! Don't you know she could squish your pretty little snout?"

"Sq-sq-squish my snout?" I stammered. Then I FAINTED.

TOO MUCH DARKNESS!

When I came to, I was in the helicopter again. Bruce was leaning over me. "Wake up, **Cheese Puff**! Come on, wake up! You never were in any real **DANGER**. I was always near you, ready to come to the **RESCUE**."

He slapped me hard on the back and continued, "You know, you're really a cheesehead, **Cheesehead**! Just give me a few more days and I'll make a **real mouse** out of you! Don't worry your pretty little snout about anything, **OK**? Leave everything to me."

"O-O-OK, but I'm not sure if I **TRUST** you. . . . Wh-wh-where are you taking me?"

"Where your worst **FEARS** will become reality: a cave!"

A CAVE?! Hmm, it couldn't be worse

CAVE EXPLORATION EQUIPMENT

PROTECTIVE HELMET

PROTECTIVE FULL-BODY SUIT

FLASHLIGHT

GLOVES

RUBBER BOOTS

CAVES

Caves are underground cavities that are created naturally by the corrosion and erosion of soil.

Although caves were used by ancient people for shelter, they are naturally inhospitable. They are usually cold, very damp, and very, **very** dark!

Speleology is the science that studies caves, their origins, and their characteristics. To explore a cave, you must bring the proper equipment.

than the JUNGLE ... could it?

An hour or two later, we were inside a **dark** cave, inching our way along a LOOOOOONG, muddy underground passage.

I couldn't see a thing! Imagine the darkest night you've ever seen, then multiply that by a thousand. **IT WAS COMPLETELY, 100 PERCENT PITCH-BLACK!** My flashlight **LIT** only a little space ahead of me.

I was trying VERY HARD to remain calm. I

reminded myself: *I'm not alone. Bruce is here. He knows how to get out of* **TROUBLE**.

As we trudged through the **mud**, Bruce warned me, "Better keep an eye out, **CHAMP**. It's very easy to get **lost** in a cave. You've got to stay **NEAR ME** at all times. If you take the wrong tunnel, you could get lost. And if you do, that's the end of you. If we're lucky, we'll find your **BONES** hundreds and hundreds of years from now. . . ."

"I-I-I don't plan to lose you!" I assured him.

"Be very careful of your **flashlight**. Don't drop it, or you'll be a **DEAD MOUSE!**"

"I-I-I don't have the slightest intention of dropping my flashlight," I assured him.

"Very good, **Cheesehead**. By the way, you remembered to bring the package with the **extra** flashlight and batteries, right?"

"Wha-a-a-t? What **PACKAGE**? What extra **flashlight**? What extra **BATTERIES**?" I was so worried, I stood up and smacked my snout against the stalactite hanging above me. The **LIGHT** on my helmet went out.

Suddenly, it was quiet. **Too quiet.**

Bruce had **disappeared**!

I screamed, "**Bruce, where are you?**"

There was no answer. Only **DEAD SILENCE**.

I was lost in the caves!

I was alone.
ALONE!
I was scared.
So very, very,
very scared!

Then I did the most idiotic thing I could have done: I began to wander through the tunnels. I WANDERED...AND WANDERED... AND WANDERED...AND WANDERED...

"Luckily, my **flashlight** is working," I reminded myself.

But just then, my flashlight flickered out. With horror, I remembered I didn't have any extra **BATTERIES**!

I was plunged into complete **DARKNESS**.

Now I knew how the **three BLiND Mice** must've felt. And it was dreadful!

I rolled up in a corner and began sobbing. After a few minutes, I tried to pull myself together. I began to sing a little **song**. It was perfect for my current situation.

After what seemed like **forever**, Bruce **FOUND** me. He had heard me **singing**!

I'M A CALM MOUSE

You know I try to be a calm mouse—
I like to stay in my own little house.
I don't enjoy taking any risks—
I DEFINITELY don't like being seasick!

I'm happiest in my own cozy mouse hole,
Glued to the fridge, eating cheese from a bowl.
I'm not a supermouse—in fact, I'm a wimp.
I'm afraid of everything, even sea shrimp!

If you mention cats, I'll start to yelp,
And I'll scamper away, shouting for help.
But as long as we're together, I'll try to be brave—
Just don't leave me alone in a dark, spooky cave!

"Good for you, **Cheesehead**!" he cried. "You were smart to **sing**! Otherwise, I never would have found you. Hundreds of years from now, if we were lucky, we'd have discovered your 𝔹𝕆ℕ𝔼𝕊. . . ."

I stopped listening. I just followed without a **squeak** as he guided me to the cave's exit and back to our **TENT**.

I was **BEYOND** tired. I was **exhausted**!

I slipped into the sleeping bag up to my ears, and sank into a

DEEEEEEEEEEEEEEP SLEEEEEEEP.

TOO MUCH STRESS!

Unfortunately, just a few minutes later, Bruce BURST into the tent and woke me up.

"Go away, Bruce!" I said, covering my snout with my paws. "I need to sleep!"

"Not now, CHAMP! I've got lots to tell you." And with that, he started CHATTERING about anything and everything he could think of. He was so annoying! I realized he was deliberately trying to *irritate* me.

This time, I was about to lose my patience.

WAS THIS ANOTHER TEST? HE WAS PUTTING ME UNDER TREMENDOUS STRESS!

He was starting to drive me crazy. First he said I was a 'fraidy mouse (which we all know is true). But then he began making

fun of *The Rodent's Gazette,* saying he found *The Daily Rat* much more enjoyable. Then he said I was lucky to have such a great family (which is true), but that they deserved much better than a STINKY cheeserat like me.

He went on like this for HOURS and HOURS. I tried to stay calm, but finally I EXPLODED. I couldn't take it anymore. I BLew uP Like a cheese casserole that's Been Left in the microwave too Long.

Bruce shook his snout. "You've learned a lot, Cheese Puff. However, you're still a little WEAK when it comes to your nerves, eh? Not to worry, though, we'll fix this little problem, too. Let me explain how and why one should keep calm in every situation."

I was too weak to ARGUE (though believe me, I wanted to!). My explosion had used up my last ounce of energy.

HOW AND WHY TO KEEP CALM IN EVERY SITUATION

Did someone get you angry?
Did you lose your patience?
Did you blow up?

Follow Bruce's advice on how to keep calm.
KEEP YOUR HEAD ABOVE WATER AND INHALE!

1. Breathe deeply.

2. Count to ten before saying or doing anything.

3. Figure out what made you angry.

4. Ask yourself if the anger you feel
   is appropriate to the situation.

   GUARANTEED CHEESY RESULTS!

5. Remember: It's not worth getting mad
   over every little thing that doesn't go your way.

6. Once you understand the problem,
   find a solution!

THE SURVIVAL
COURSE IS . . .

At dawn the following day, an ear-splitting scream woke me up.

"Cheeseheeeeeeeeeeeeeeeeeeeeeead!"

I jumped up and ran outside, ready to face any situation.

What was waiting for me this time?

What DANGER lurked ahead?

What EMERGENCY?

What ADVENTURE?

Bruce was standing outside the tent with his paws folded. He STARED at me for a long moment. At last he SHOUTED, "Now, listen to me!

"The survival course is over!"

I was flabbergasted.

"Wh-what did you say? The course is **OVER**?"

"Yes!" Bruce answered.

"No more **cold**?"

"No."

"No more **HEAT**?"

"No."

"No more **hard work**?"

"No."

"No more **hunger**, **thirst**, and **DARKNESS**?"

"No, no, and no!"

Bruce hung an enormouse **GOLD MEDAL** around my neck. Then, for the first time, he smiled at me and uttered two precious words: **"WELL DONE!"**

I answered with one grateful, sincere word: **"THANKS!"**

THE REAL SURVIVAL TEST IS HERE AND NOW!

Bruce plucked a tuft of fur off my ear and pawed me a sheet of **paper**.

"Make good use of it, Cheese Puff! You'll need it!" Bruce strode off toward a nearby hotel. We were going to spend the night there before returning to Mouse Island.

I didn't have the energy to read what he had handed me. I **dragged** myself to the hotel and crawled to my room.

I headed to the bathroom, slipped into a hot **BATH**, and tried to relax my aching muscles.

I began to read the sheet of paper Bruce gave me. It was a *diploma*! My whiskers quivered with **emotion**. I almost burst into

SURVIVAL COURSE
Diploma

I, BRUCE HYENA, DO SOLEMNLY SWEAR THAT GERONIMO STILTON OVERCAME THE FOLLOWING CHALLENGES:

- the heat of the Sahara
- the chill of the North Pole
- the terror of the jungle
- the darkness of the caves

I CERTIFY THAT MR. GERONIMO STILTON, ALSO KNOWN AS CHEESE PUFF, HAS COMPLETED MY SURVIVAL COURSE.

Bruce Hyena

DON'T FORGET:

1. The desert taught you that no matter how hard your daily problems are, the important thing is to face them with the right attitude.
2. Our polar trek taught you to never give up. Be optimistic and have faith in yourself.
3. Life is an opportunity for growth. It is also an opportunity to make new friends, just like you did in the jungle, ha-ha-ha!
4. Finally, remember that this is your life — the only one you'll ever have. It's the spice you give it that makes it exciting. Singing in the cave is just the beginning!

In other words, the real survival test is here and now, every day!

tears. I had done it!

I had passed the test, and I was so **glad** it was over!

While I was reflecting on the last few days, I decided I was a little hungry. I finished my **BATH** and ordered a snack from room service: cheesy spaghetti. I gobbled down the food, savoring each **DELICIOUSLY** cheesy bite. Then I scampered into bed, got comfortable, and mumbled, "I'm just gonna close my eyes for a quick ratnap ... a little rest ...

ZZZZ....ZZZZ...ZZZZ

ZZZZZ . . . ZZZZZZZZZ . . . ZZZZZ . . .
ZZZZZZZZ . . . ZZZZZZ . . . ZZZZZ . . .
ZZZZZZZZ. . . ."

I woke up TWENTY-FOUR hours later.
Holey cheese! That was some **NAP**!

That was some nap!

AN AWESOME EXPERIENCE

We headed for home that same day. We arrived in *New Mouse City* the following morning. I decided to go straight to **The Rodent's Gazette**. I couldn't wait to see my family and all my friends!

I said hello to everybody, went into my office, sat at my desk, opened my appointment book, and turned on my computer.

There I was . . . back to my **DAILY ROUTINE**! It felt good.

Then **I SIGHED**.

I had experienced so many **adventures**!

I had worked **hard**, felt fear, and several times I'd thought I'd never make it out alive.

But now, thinking it over . . .

Well...
so...
maybe...
perhaps...
I had to admit
that it was an
awesome experience!

But there was no time for reminiscing. The door to my office **slammed** open, and my sister Thea burst in.

At first I thought she had come to *welcome* me home, but I could tell she had something on her mind. "Geronimo, have you heard the **news**?" she asked, a look of WOrry on her snout.

Bewildered, I shook my head. "What news?"

She turned on the **TV**: There was a newsflash on. "Here is the very latest news! A major **STORM** has just hit the northern part of Mouse Island, near Blue Dolphin Bay. We do not yet know the extent of the **DAMAGE**. We'll keep you posted with a **minute-by-minute** report!"

I sprang to my paws. The situation was very **serious**! Somebody had to do something *right away*!

The phone rang. It was the Honorable Ratmouse, New Mouse City's mayor.

"Geronimo, my friend, I need your help. We have to do something *right away*! Emergency workers are **RUSHING** up north, but we need all the help we can get!"

"I know, Mr. Mayor," I said. "I'll send out a **NEWSBLAST** from *The Rodent's Gazette* website to ask for volunteers. But I really don't know how else

I can help you. I'm a NEWSPAPER PUBLISHER. I don't know how to organize EMERGENCY relief."

"I understand," the mayor said SADLY. "It doesn't matter. I was hoping that you . . . well, let me know if you think of something."

I felt terrible. I was sorry to disappoint the mayor. I hung up the phone and put my head on my desk. How could I help? There were too many things that needed to be done. The job was TOO BIG for a single mouse!

Even Thea was at a LOSS. And my sister is one of the world's BiggeSt know-it-alls!

NEVER GIVE UP

If there was one thing I learned through my experience with Bruce, it was **to never give up**! I thought, *Maybe one rodent can't do much on his own, but many friends together can do* **a lot***!*

I jumped up and shouted, "We can do it!"

I called all my coworkers into an **extra-urgent** meeting. In a few minutes everyone was there, out of breath and worried. Once everyone was assembled in the meeting room, I jumped on a chair and said, "Friends, I have called you here because something **really serious** has happened."

Then I waited silently. Everyone's eyes were **FIXED** on me. I looked at each mouse, **ONE BY ONE**, and went on.

"Today the **mayor** asked for our help. A huge **STORM** has hit the northern part of Mouse Island."

Everyone murmured, "A what?"

"It's not **possible**!"

"There's never been a big storm on that part of the island!"

"Unfortunately, it's **true**!" I continued. "We need to act now! We need a lot of volunteers. Who can help?"

Everyone answered with one voice.

"Meeeeee!"

I was moved. "Thank you, everyone. I was sure I could count on you."

Trying to remain calm and steady, I began assigning tasks to everyone.

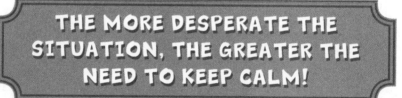

THE MORE DESPERATE THE SITUATION, THE GREATER THE NEED TO KEEP CALM!

Watching me work, Thea said, "Geronimo, are you sure you're feeling OK? You don't look like yourself. You almost look like . . .

I smiled at her. "Don't get your tail in a twist, Thea. I'm still ME! If I look different, it's all because of Bruce and his advice."

I called all the contacts in my address book: Every one of them was willing to HELP OUT!

I'M NOT A
SUPERMOUSE!

I decided to rush out a special edition of the paper. We'd report the latest on the **STORM**, and urge all the rodents on Mouse Island to do their part during the **EMERGENCY** by donating money, food, clothing, blankets, medicine, and transportation. We'd make it clear we welcomed advice as well as donations of time and **MATERIALS**.

When I called the mayor to tell him what I intended to do, he was very **moved**.

"Geronimo, you never fail to amaze me. What happened to you? You've changed. You almost seem like **A SUPERMOUSE**!"

I smiled to myself, thinking about what

Bruce had taught me, and answered, "No, **Mr. Mayor**, I'm not a supermouse. I'm still me: *Geronimo Stilton*! But recently I've learned a few lessons on facing **ADVERSITY**."

I called my family and friends and asked them to come to the office. Each of my co-workers did the same. In a short time, there were more than fifty of us.

At first, **THERE WAS TOTAL CHAOS**! So I divided everyone into groups according to ability, then picked someone to head each group.

The **special edition** of *The Rodent's Gazette* was printed in record time! Thanks to **volunteers**, it was quickly distributed throughout the city.

My grandfather, William Shortpaws, looked

me in the eyes and said, "Good for you, grandson! I'm almost beginning to think I was right to **TRUST** you with the newspaper. . . . You've become a **real mouse**!"

A few hours later, a small **CROWD** had gathered outside **The Rodent's Gazette**. I opened the window and saw rodents of all ages in all sorts of **bizarre** vehicles: a tractor trailer, a skateboard, a little red wagon. Everyone had brought something: blankets, food, medicine. It was an **amazing** display of friendship and solidarity.

We loaded the provisions and **supplies** onto the tractor trailer, and our group of fearless rodents was ready to take off for the northern coast of Mouse Island.

Grandfather William announced: **"I'LL GIVE THE ORDERS!"**

Thea, Trap, and I stared at one another in

dismay. Then we all started SQUEAKING at once.

"No, thank you, Grandfather, please, we don't want to **bother** you!" I said.

"Grandfather, why don't you stay here and rest instead?" Thea said. "We need someone to supervise operations at headquarters."

But Grandfather IGNORED us. He scampered onto the bus that was leading the supply vehicles. Thea, Trap, Benjamin, Bruce, and I quickly scrambled in after him. Grandfather immediately began **BARKING** out commands. "OK, this is going to be a long trip, so let's lay down some RULES here! The following are **STRICTLY PROHIBITED** on board this bus:

· **Squeaking loudly.**
· **Singing rock music.**
· **Sticking Cheesy Chews under your seat.**

· **Picking your snout.**
· **Picking your neighbor's snout.**

"Finally, I hope everyone brought a good BOOK! Let's start reading, and we'll each give an **oral report** at the end of the ride." With that, he pulled out a book and started reading.

Thea and I **LOOKED** at each other and shrugged.

"Did you bring a book?" she asked.

"No, I forgot —" I began.

But Grandfather cut me off. "Geronimo! What did I tell you about squeaking loudly!" He shook his snout sadly. "And just when I was thinking you were turning into a **REAL MOUSE**!"

It was a very **looooong** trip.

Up To My
Whiskers in Mud!

When we reached the northernmost part
of Mouse Island, we saw there was a lot of
work to do. The **MUDDY WATERS** of the river
had **Risen** almost to the top of the banks.
Towns were in danger of being flooded!

Something had to be done **IMMEDIATELY**!
But what? I didn't know where to start!

Bruce crossed his paws and gazed at me seriously. "Assess, decide, and act!"

I thought for a SECOND and knew what to do. "Listen up, everyone!" I called. All the rodents huddled around. "We need to reinforce the riverbanks. Let's concentrate our resources on stopping the river from SPILLING OVER. Together, we can do it!"

There was a roar of approval. "Yeeeees! We can do it!"

To keep the river in check, rodents filled

Here.

Let me help you.

sacks with sand. Others used bulldozers to pile up masses of **ROCKS**, bundles of **WOOD**, and **tree trunks** by the side of the river.

Then we made a rodent chain to pass the **SAND** and **ROCKS** from paw to paw. We began to build a **BARRIER** along the river.

Soon we were up to our whiskers in mud. Though the rain had stopped, our clothes were dripping wet, and our paws were aching. But we were filled with **DETERMINATION**.

As we worked, I decided to sing my favorite song, *"I'm a Calm Mouse!"* Soon, a few other rodents around me joined in.

In no time, we were all singing. Together, we were truly extraordinary mice!

I caught Thea's eye. She winked at me and cried, "Friends together! Mice forever!"

RODENTS WITH BIG HEARTS!

As we were **singing**, a ray of sun peeked out of the clouds, and a breathtaking RAINBOW stretched across the sky.

We returned to our work with newfound energy. Soon we found that WE HAD DONE IT! We had stopped the waters of the river from rushing over the banks: The towns were SAVED!

There was a lot more to do, but the worst was over. It would take an entire book to tell you what all those rodents with big hearts did: They cleaned MUD from houses, they comforted children and the elderly, they made HOT meals and cold sandwiches, they spoke *gently and compassionately* to mice who'd lost their homes. They were **AMAZING**!

I'll tell you one last thing.

I decided to record the song we all sang together, the song that gave us such **STRENGTH** and **COURAGE**. It was an enormouse success!

That's the **truth**, or my name isn't *Geronimo Stilton*!

Want to read my next adventure?
I can't wait to tell you all about it!

THE GIANT
DIAMOND ROBBERY

I, Geronimo Stilton, am no sportsmouse. But
that didn't stop Grandfather William from
dragging me to a golf tournament so I could
be his caddie! Once I arrived, who should
I bump into but my friend Kornelius Von
Kickpaw, a.k.a. Special Agent 00K. Someone
was plotting to steal the Super Mouse Cup,
and it was up to me and Kornelius to crack
the case!

And don't miss any of my other fabumouse adventures!

#1 LOST TREASURE OF THE EMERALD EYE

#2 THE CURSE OF THE CHEESE PYRAMID

#3 CAT AND MOUSE IN A HAUNTED HOUSE

#4 I'M TOO FOND OF MY FUR!

#5 FOUR MICE DEEP IN THE JUNGLE

#6 PAWS OFF, CHEDDARFACE!

#7 RED PIZZAS FOR A BLUE COUNT

#8 ATTACK OF THE BANDIT CATS

#9 A FABUMOUSE VACATION FOR GERONIMO

#10 ALL BECAUSE OF A CUP OF COFFEE

#11 IT'S HALLOWEEN, YOU 'FRAIDY MOUSE!

#12 MERRY CHRISTMAS, GERONIMO!

#13 THE PHANTOM OF THE SUBWAY

#14 THE TEMPLE OF THE RUBY OF FIRE

#15 THE MONA MOUSA CODE

#16 A CHEESE-COLORED CAMPER

#17 WATCH YOUR WHISKERS, STILTON!

#18 SHIPWRECK ON THE PIRATE ISLANDS

#19 MY NAME IS STILTON, GERONIMO STILTON

#20 SURF'S UP, GERONIMO!

#21 THE WILD, WILD WEST

#22 THE SECRET OF CACKLEFUR CASTLE

A CHRISTMAS TALE

#23 VALENTINE'S DAY DISASTER

#24 FIELD TRIP TO NIAGARA FALLS

#25 THE SEARCH FOR SUNKEN TREASURE

#26 THE MUMMY WITH NO NAME

#27 THE CHRISTMAS TOY FACTORY

#28 WEDDING CRASHER

#29 DOWN AND OUT DOWN UNDER

#30 THE MOUSE ISLAND MARATHON

#31 THE MYSTERIOUS CHEESE THIEF

CHRISTMAS CATASTROPHE

#32 VALLEY OF THE GIANT SKELETONS

#33 GERONIMO AND THE GOLD MEDAL MYSTERY

#34 GERONIMO STILTON, SECRET AGENT

#35 A VERY MERRY CHRISTMAS

#36 GERONIMO'S VALENTINE

#37 THE RACE ACROSS AMERICA

#38 A FABUMOUSE SCHOOL ADVENTURE

#39 SINGING SENSATION

#40 THE KARATE MOUSE

#41 MIGHTY MOUNT KILIMANJARO

#42 THE PECULIAR PUMPKIN THIEF

#43 I'M NOT A SUPERMOUSE!

Coming soon!

#44 THE GIANT DIAMOND ROBBERY

Don't miss these very special editions!

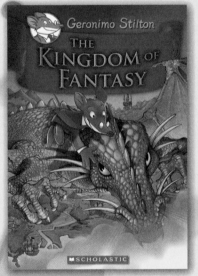

THE KINGDOM OF FANTASY

THE QUEST FOR PARADISE:
THE RETURN TO THE KINGDOM OF FANTASY

If you like my brother's books,
check out the next adventure
of the Thea Sisters!

THEA STILTON AND THE
MYSTERY IN PARIS

When Colette invites her friends to come home with her to Paris for spring break, the five mice are delighted. While they're in France, they'll even get to attend Colette's fashion-designer friend Julie's runway show at the Eiffel Tower! But soon after the Thea Sisters arrive, Julie's designs are stolen. Will the five mice be able to catch the thief in time to save the fashion show?

Be sure to check out these other exciting Thea Sisters adventures:

THEA STILTON AND THE DRAGON'S CODE

THEA STILTON AND THE MOUNTAIN OF FIRE

THEA STILTON AND THE GHOST OF THE SHIPWRECK

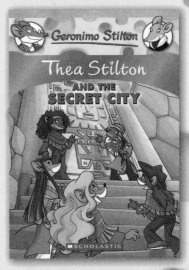

THEA STILTON AND THE SECRET CITY

ABOUT THE AUTHOR

Born in New Mouse City, Mouse Island, **GERONIMO STILTON** is Rattus Emeritus of Mousomorphic Literature and of Neo-Ratonic Comparative Philosophy. For the past twenty years, he has been running *The Rodent's Gazette*, New Mouse City's most widely read daily newspaper.

Stilton was awarded the Ratitzer Prize for his scoops on *The Curse of the Cheese Pyramid* and *The Search for Sunken Treasure*. He has also received the Andersen 2000 Prize for Personality of the Year. One of his bestsellers won the 2002 eBook Award for world's best ratlings' electronic book. His works have been published all over the globe.

In his spare time, Mr. Stilton collects antique cheese rinds and plays golf. But what he most enjoys is telling stories to his nephew Benjamin.

THE RODENT'S GAZETTE

1. Main entrance
2. Printing presses (where the books and newspaper are printed)
3. Accounts department
4. Editorial room (where the editors, illustrators, and designers work)
5. Geronimo Stilton's office
6. Storage space for Geronimo's books

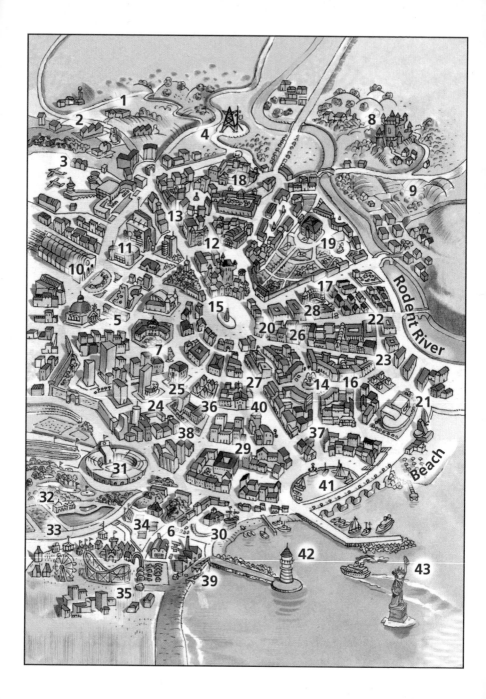

Map of New Mouse City

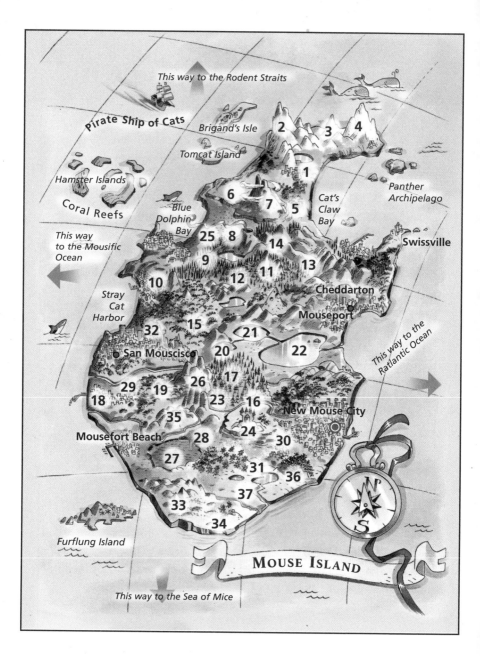

This way to the Rodent Straits

Pirate Ship of Cats

Brigand's Isle

Tomcat Island

Hamster Islands

Coral Reefs

Blue Dolphin Bay

This way to the Mousific Ocean

Panther Archipelago

Cat's Claw Bay

Swissville

Stray Cat Harbor

Cheddarton

Mouseport

San Mouscisco

This way to the Ratlantic Ocean

Mousefort Beach

New Mouse City

Furflung Island

MOUSE ISLAND

This way to the Sea of Mice

Map of Mouse Island

1. Big Ice Lake
2. Frozen Fur Peak
3. Slipperyslopes Glacier
4. Coldcreeps Peak
5. Ratzikistan
6. Transratania
7. Mount Vamp
8. Roastedrat Volcano
9. Brimstone Lake
10. Poopedcat Pass
11. Stinko Peak
12. Dark Forest
13. Vain Vampires Valley
14. Goose Bumps Gorge
15. The Shadow Line Pass
16. Penny Pincher Castle
17. Nature Reserve Park
18. Las Ratayas Marinas
19. Fossil Forest
20. Lake Lake
21. Lake Lakelake
22. Lake Lakelakelake
23. Cheddar Crag
24. Cannycat Castle
25. Valley of the Giant Sequoia
26. Cheddar Springs
27. Sulfurous Swamp
28. Old Reliable Geyser
29. Vole Vale
30. Ravingrat Ravine
31. Gnat Marshes
32. Munster Highlands
33. Mousehara Desert
34. Oasis of the Sweaty Camel
35. Cabbagehead Hill
36. Rattytrap Jungle
37. Rio Mosquito

Dear mouse friends,
Thanks for reading, and farewell
till the next book.
It'll be another whisker-licking-good
adventure, and that's a promise!

Geronimo Stilton